AVALANCHE

First edition 1998

Library of Congress Cataloging-in-Publication Data
Rosen, Michael J., date.
Avalanche / written by Michael J. Rosen ;
illustrated by David Butler. — 1st ed.
p.   cm.
Summary: A rhyming alphabet book in which a boy tosses a
snowball to his dog and starts an avalanche that engulfs the
entire universe until it has to reverse itself and become
a snowball again, ending up in the dog's mouth.
ISBN 0-7636-0589-1
[1. Avalanches — Fiction. 2. Dogs — Fiction. 3. Snow — Fiction.
4. Stories in rhyme. 5. Alphabet.] I. Butler, David, date, ill. II. Title.
PZ8.3.R7223Av   1998
[E] — dc21   98-14050

2 4 6 8 10 9 7 5 3 1

Printed in Italy

This book was typeset in Myriad.
The pictures were done in collage and mixed media.

Candlewick Press
2067 Massachusetts Avenue
Cambridge, Massachusetts 02140

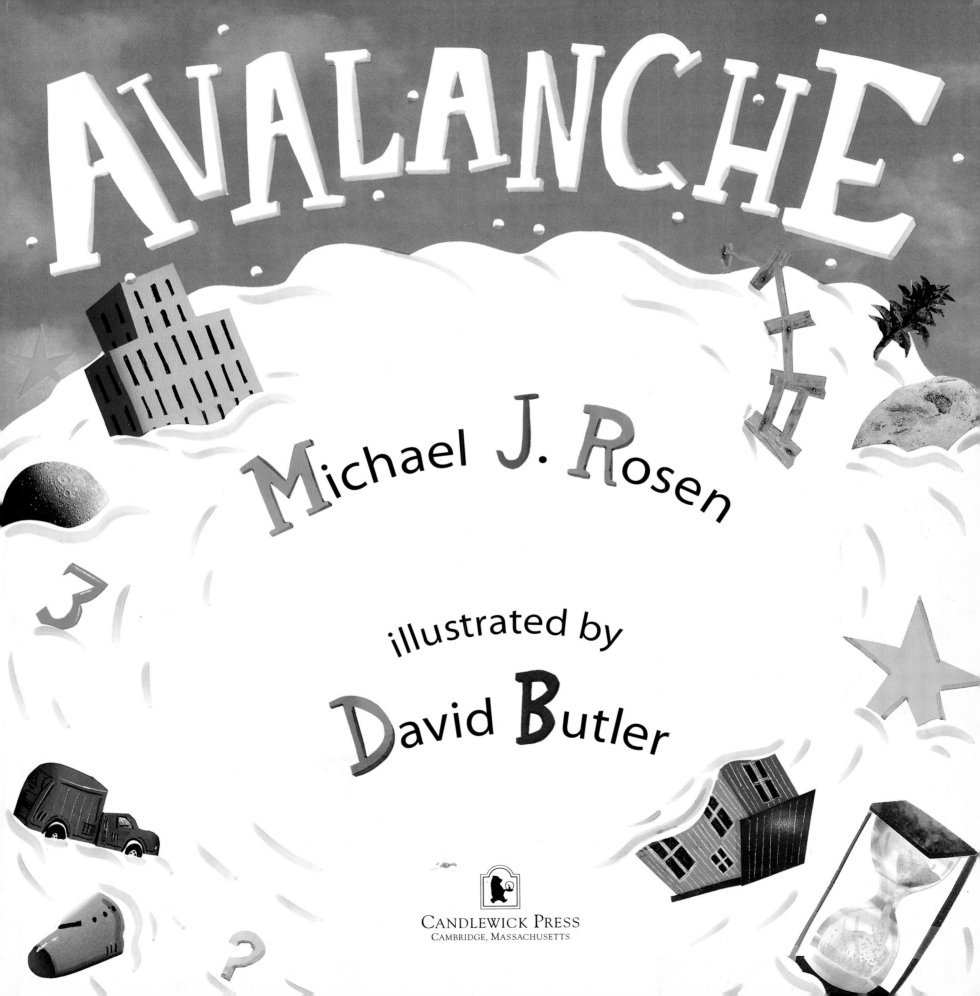

AVALANCHE

Michael J. Rosen

illustrated by

David Butler

CANDLEWICK PRESS
CAMBRIDGE, MASSACHUSETTS

Once there was an **A**valanche

that started out quite small.

It all began when **B**obby tossed

a harmless-looking ball. . . .

The snowball sailed across the yard and struck a Cat-food can.

It caught the Doghouse in its path as though it had a plan.

The ball uprooted Evergreens
and widened, wobbled, fattened.
It toppled someone's four-foot Fence,
which froze around it, flattened.

The Greens' garage fell under next
(both cars were gone — what luck!),
and then the snowball overturned
a giant garbage truck.

Hey! What's the big idea?" yelled Irene, the traffic cop. The icy orb absorbed her words, and, no, it didn't stop.

Lift off! The snow unearthed a **J**et
and took it for a drive.
The frosty **K**ingdom touched the clouds —
that snowball was alive!

It blotted up a lengthy Lake,
then smooshed a Mountain range.

Each Nation that the ball engulfed,
it wholly rearranged.

NORTH POLE

Oceans doused the growing globe
and iced our total Planet,
just like prehistoric times
when glaciers overran it.

and bygone Rainbows float along
whose lives were short and sweet.

The Stars within the zodiac
lit on the snowball's brow,

TUESDAY

and so did **T**ime — like Then, Someday, Too Late!, So Soon?, and Now.

What else was left to feed the ball?
It filled the Universe!
The only place that it could go
was somewhere in reverse.

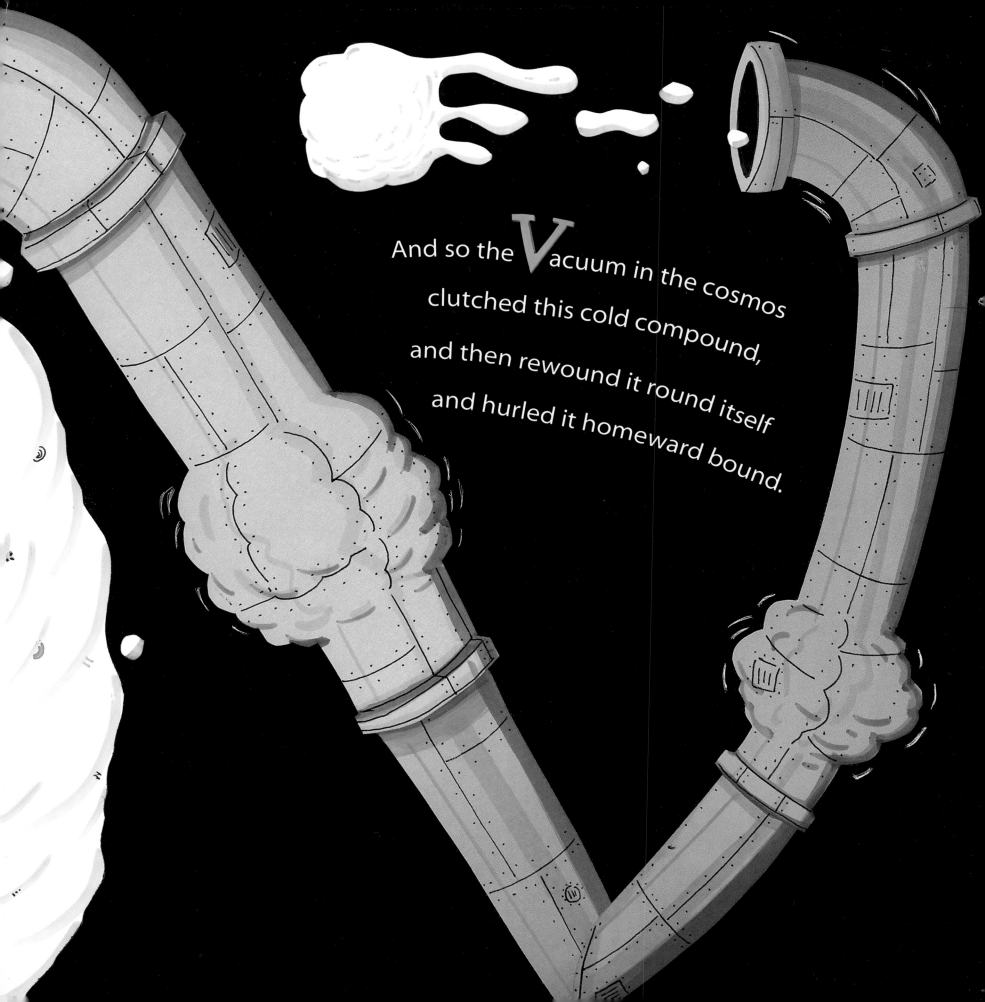

And so the Vacuum in the cosmos
clutched this cold compound,
and then rewound it round itself
and hurled it homeward bound.

With every twist something split off,

returning to our World:

Each question, ocean, lake, and jet

uncurled and downward swirled.

X marked each spot where something stood
before the snowball's theft,

and each thing landed back in place —
or had it ever left?

As for **Y**ou, you might have seen,

or maybe might have heard,

the alphabet that's rolled inside

this avalanche of words.

When, finally, that small white ball

descended to the snow,

Zippy, Bobby's dog, he caught it!

Gadzooks! What a throw!

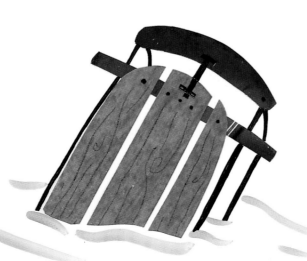